ERMANNO CRISTINI
LUIGI PURICELLI

IN THE WOODS

IN GRAPHIC COLLABORATION WITH RENATO PEGORARO

Summer is not quite over,
fall hasn't quite arrived,
and we are walking in the woods.

Step softly now,
and you will see some of the creatures that live here.
Shh---don't frighten them away.
Who knows? ... If you keep your eyes open,
and look very carefully,
you just might see them all!

pocket in front

Copyright, © 1983, Verlag Neugebauer Press, Salzburg.
Introductory text copyright, © 1983, Neugebauer Press USA, Inc.
Published in USA by Picture Book Studio USA, an imprint of Neugebauer Press USA.
Distributed by Alphabet Press, Natick, MA.
Distributed in Canada by Grolier Ltd., Toronto.
Published in UK by Neugebauer Press Publishing Ltd., London, WC1.
Distributed by A&C Black PLC., London.

All Rights Reserved.
Printed in Austria by Druckhaus Nonntal, Salzburg.
ISBN O-907234-31-3

Library of Congress Cataloging in Publication Data
Cristini, Ermanno.
In the woods.
Summary: Presents a wordless panorama of the animals, plants, insects,
and flowers of the forest.
(1. Forests and forestry-Fiction. 2. Stories without words
I. Puricelli, Luigi.) II. Title.
PZ7.C86966Ip 1983 (E) 83-8153
ISBN O-907234-31-3